a poetic novel

THE CHOSEN

GORDON BOSTIC

ISBN (Paperback)978-1-962733-99-1
ISBN (E-book): 978-1-962733-98-4

Printed in United States of America

First paper back edition September 2023
Book design by Writer's Way Solutions
publish by Writer's Way Solutions
www.writerswaysolutions.com

Dedication

*To my wife, Susan, for her love,
support and putting up with me.*

Contents

The Town

The town had been nothing special.
Some may say, typical.
A small slice of America
Where nothing's critical.

Whatever problems they may have
They'd get to in due time.
For it's a quiet little town
That rarely saw a crime.

There were no nightclubs or hotspots
Though drinking did occur.
Most notably on Friday nights
When their work was secure.

Their churches filled on Sunday morns
For thankfulness and praise
That their town had been so peaceful
Where children could be raised.

Though scandals rose from time to time
They're few and far between
'Cause small towns rarely had secrets
As ev'rything is seen.

The Runaway

He simply was a runaway
Who wandered into town.
Then found that he was penniless
As luck had dwindled down.

A shopkeeper, whose name was Lou,
Had dared to take him in.
Who never asked about his past
Or where it was he'd been.

The shopkeeper gave him a job
And, also, room and board.
Lou claimed it was not charity
But for his work reward.

Though now he had a second chance
To get his life on track.
If he'd simply take advantage
And choose to not look back.

The Mayor

For the first time since its founding
Their mayor was female.
Her election was surprising
Because she'd done so well.

The fact that she had not campaigned
May should have questions raised.
But none had found it curious
A new trail had been blazed.

Stranger still that her opponents,
Who challenged and campaigned,
Had never questioned the results
Nor secretly complained.

Though she never would admit it
She felt a little shame.
For she'd been one of the Chosen
And dared to rig the game.

The Shopkeeper's Daughter

Lou's daughter's name was Marybeth
And she was somewhat shy.
Rob thought she was a pretty girl
Which Lou could not deny.

She rarely ever spoke to him
Unless she had no choice.
And even then, it was not clear
So soft had been her voice.

He'd tried to introduce himself
But she'd not seemed to care.
As though she never noticed that
He even had been there.

Although he'd seen the random glance
When she would look his way.
Whatever she had thought of him
She had no will to say.

Strange Occurrences

Throughout the town's long history
Some odd things had occurred.
Though most of them had not been bad
Some trauma they endured.

The child that fell into the well
Who'd somehow gotten out.
The tornado that had missed them
After it changed its route.

The child that fell into the pool
Yet, somehow had survived.
These outcomes were not natural
But also not contrived.

The people had felt fortunate
In luck that they possessed.
Though the cause of their good fortune
Not one of them had guessed.

The Chosen

They had called themselves the chosen
As they'd come to believe
A higher force selected them
With greatness to achieve.

They believed it was their calling
To aid their fellow man.
And employ their abilities
In any way they can.

Though forced to work in secrecy
As no one was to know
What were their capabilities
They weren't allowed to show.

Some higher purpose called to them
To which they must respond.
For it was their prime directive
That came from the beyond.

But man has shown a true distrust
Of what he can't define.
And those who were the chosen few
Had clearly crossed that line.

The Preacher

The preacher who was new in town
Believed in the occult.
And ev'ry Sunday he would preach
About their evil cult.

Each Sunday he would rant and rave
That witches had been real.
As though he was obsessed by it
So strong was his appeal.

He claimed he'd first discovered them
While serving in Dale Glen.
Where those they found were forced to pay
In answer to their sin.

Since then his mission had been clear
And he believed divine.
To look for witches where he went
By rules he would define.

He claimed he's ever vigilant
To see through their disguise.
For witches were a wicked breed
As truth they did despise.

A New Beginning

Though Rob was truly likeable
His life, so far, a waste.
For choices that he found he made
He did not wish to face.

But here he'd found stability
And, maybe, a new home.
As he seemed to be accepted
And lost his will to roam.

They gave him opportunity
To turn his life around.
And here he had found happiness
Which he had not yet found.

And, also, there was Marybeth
With whom he was intrigued.
Though attempts for her attention
Had left him quite fatigued.

The Stranger

No one in town expected him,
Thus, none had known his name.
There were none who knew his purpose
Nor why it was he came.

He had simply been a stranger
They assumed would pass through.
For theirs had been a little town
With nothing much to do.

He hardly spoke to anyone
Unless there was a need.
And when he spoke it was direct
As smiles he'd not concede.

There was a certain air to him
Where nervousness would spew.
As though he looked into your soul
And all your secrets knew.

But one without identity
Is sure to raise a flag.
For in a small community
The tongues were sure to wag.

His Acolytes

The Preacher had his acolytes
Who hung on ev'ry word.
They'd become his inner circle
Believing all they heard.

They completely were devoted
And married to the cause.
They did whatever he would ask
Without question or pause.

His acolytes would stir the crowds
That they would infiltrate.
All responding to his message
And propagating hate.

And his acolytes would serve him
In any way they could
Without any hesitation
To what was bad or good.

The Dinner

One morning before opening
Lou turned to Rob and said
His wife wished he'd come for dinner
So, she'd make sure he's fed.

When Marybeth answered the door
Rob smiled and said hello.
But Marybeth stood dumbfounded
As shock she seemed to show.

Then Lou had told him to come in
And meet the family.
Rob gently had pushed her aside
So, he could gain entry.

At dinner she'd not said a word
As all she did was stare.
As if she could not phantom why
Her father brought him there.

Then Rob had helped Michelle clean up
Before he had to leave.
While Marybeth seemed to believe
Her parents were naïve.

The Old Age Home

There was no sign there was a crime
Until they went inside.
Where they found all its residents
Had simply up and died.

Although it seemed unusual
No crime had been confirmed.
For after all they all were old
And most of them informed.

But also dead were orderlies
And all its personnel
Without a sign there'd been foul play
Which did not sit that well.

They refused to call it murder
Although they found it strange
The cause had not been obvious
And did not seem short-range.

Random Thoughts

After he left, while walking home
Some thoughts flashed through his mind.
Lou and Michelle were nice to him
And proven to be kind.

Though Lou seemed to be much older
Than was his wife, Michelle.
All in all, they had seemed happy
And appeared to do well.

Lou married way above himself.
Michelle was beautiful.
But it's their daughter, Marybeth,
Whom he had been mindful.

It seemed that she'd not trusted him
Though he could not say why.
She barely ever spoke to him
And mostly passed him by.

So why he was intrigued with her
He could not really say.
As though she placed a spell a him
That would not go away.

A Creature of the Night

He was a creature of the night
Who to the shadows held.
If ever he was in a crowd
It's to the back he'd meld.

It seemed that he was ev'rywhere
And yet, no one could say
That he had been there at the time
The façade broke away.

There clearly was no evidence
To show that he was there.
And they could find no witnesses
Who were willing to swear.

The Preacher claimed that he had known
But he, they had ignored.
It was clearly due to witchcraft
But that went unexplored.

Miss Blackstone

Miss Blackstone was the old school marm
Who came to town and stayed.
But she never found a husband
So, wound up an old maid.

She'd become an institution
As she'd been there for years.
She had been their inspiration
And had allayed their fears.

Miss Blackstone was the cornerstone
Of the community.
She had been loved by all in town
Who'd trust her honesty.

But there had been a change in her
That most did not discern.
If it had been more obvious
Perhaps they'd shown concern.

She'd taught 'most ev'ry one in town
And thus, gained their respect.
Although the secret that she kept
Not one would dare expect.

The Profile

The Preacher composed a profile
So to identify
Those he thought would be most likely
To live a witch's lie.

First, it's likely they're not married
And chose to live alone.
They'd live outside society
And friends had never known.

And there would be no beauty queens,
As they'd appear quite plain.
Some could even be disfigured
Such evil they'd contain.

He thought his profile was correct
Down to the last detail.
For all of them were truly spawned
Within the depths of hell.

While Locking Up

One night as Rob was locking up
He turned to find her there.
He asked if she had been okay
But all she did was stare.

He asked if she forgot something
But she said not a word.
She simply stood and stared at him
As though she had not heard.

Instinctively, he reached for her
But she had pulled away.
As though she was afraid of him
Although she would not say.

And then she turned and disappeared
Into the dark of night.
Whatever Marybeth had wished
He had not made it right.

Stories of the Beast

They believed it was a story
T'was contrived by their priest
Of the horrors that would happen
Should they arouse the beast.

For the beast was of pure evil
And goodness it'd despise.
But it was easy to arouse
By those who were unwise.

For the beast would feed on hatred.
As much as it could find.
So hatred was an element
That should not fill the mind.

Most thought the beast a fairy tale
To keep them all in line.
For nothing that's that terrible
Could be of God's design.

The Purpose of the Chosen

When Emmy Lou had fallen ill,
Just after she turned four.
Her doctors clearly gave up hope
Her health they could restore.

But fate had proved the doctors wrong
As slowly she improved.
When hope was all but lost to them
It seemed that fate was moved.

Then old man Winters broke his hip
After a tragic fall.
They thought it was the end of him
For chance to heal was small.

But once again a miracle
Had seemed to save the day.
It seemed that his recovery
Had been well underway.

In each case when there was a need
One Chosen had been there.
Because that was their destiny
To offer aid and care.

A Social Statement

Though ev'ryone attended church
For most it was for show.
As all in the community
Had seemed obliged to go.

It was more a social statement
Than statement of belief.
For after church they'd socialize
But that too had been brief.

It was though it was expected
As just a social norm.
Just the pattern they all followed
As all wished to conform.

Fate

He wondered what he'd stumbled on
And why he was drawn here.
For all he saw was turbulence
And a tremendous fear.

Then Marybeth had looked at him
And said to her it's clear.
She told him it's no accident
That fate had brought him here.

She believed that she'd been chosen
To face a special threat.
But what it was she had not known
At least, that is, not yet.

But something deep inside of her
Said he'd a role to play.
When fate should merely intercede
To make him pass this way.

The Johnson's Child

The Johnson's child had fallen ill
To subsequently die.
His parents had been heartbroken
And wanted to know why.

There was a sense of bitterness
That help had not arrived.
For other children who were ill
All had somehow survived.

The town expressed its sympathy
For none should have to face
The passing of a precious child
Whose love they can't replace.

There was no need the Johnson's child
Had been allowed to die.
But the power of the Chosen
One chosen did deny.

Miss Blackstone's Visit

Miss Blackstone came to visit them
And offered them support.
The Johnsons were appreciative
But caught a little short.

For there'd been something about her
That left them with a chill.
It was nothing that specific
But there had been a feel.

Since neither one grew up in town
They had not come to learn
Miss Blackstone was a cornerstone
To whom people would turn.

But when she took her leave of them
They felt a great relief.
For what she seemed to offer them
Was well beyond belief.

Once She had been Chosen

She was once one of the Chosen
They were forced to dismiss.
It seemed that she had lost her way
And lived in an abyss.

Her powers had begun to fade
The more her faith would wane.
It seemed she'd grown delusional
And bordered on insane.

The accusations that she made
They'd found total nonsense.
And it seemed that she'd found patterns
In pure coincidence.

For all the good that she had done
They felt it was a shame
That now she was reduced to this –
The ember of a flame.

The Coopers

The Coopers both were elderly
But ev'ry day they'd walk.
Most often they would cruise the park
And, sometimes, stopped to talk.

But on that fateful afternoon
They chose to walk downtown.
Where a car with no parking break
Broke free and ran them down.

The owner swore the brake was set
And could not understand
How the car was put in motion
When it had been unmanned.

Though the inspection that was made
Could find no part at fault.
So, it remained a mystery
What had caused the assault.

The Mayor's Concerns

The mayor had become concerned
The Preacher was a threat.
His rallies grew more passionate
As were the goals he set.

At first the rallies had been sparse
But over time had grown.
Although the message he relayed
Was grossly overblown.

He claimed that he had evidence
That witches do exist.
And in due time he'd gladly name
The one who topped his list.

It had been curiosity
That brought the people in.
Now with ev'ry odd occurrence
The crowds refused to thin.

The Cooper's Friends

The Coopers had been friends of theirs
So, both had been upset.
The explanation they received
Was one they'd not accept.

The Coopers had no family
So, it was left to friends
To settle on the arrangements
That finalized their ends.

He'd heard Michelle had been a mess
And Marybeth had cried.
Police called it an accident
But Lou believed they lied.

It's just a feeling that he had
That he could not explain.
But something had been left unsaid
And he thought that was plain.

The Church

Lou invited Rob to join them
As part of their journey
Next Sunday when they went to church
As a whole family.

Rob told Lou he believed in God
But not so much the church.
For when he had the need of it,
It left him in a lurch.

But, finally, he acquiesced
And, sullenly, agreed.
For they had been so kind to him
To argue he'd no need.

They sat together in a pew;
He next to Marybeth.
He barely heard what had been said
Except they spoke of death.

Rob accidently brushed her hand
But she'd not pulled away.
Instead, she let it linger there
Till it came time to pray.

The Chosen's Enemy

The Chosen had an enemy
They feared they could not tame.
For he was reckless with his words
And showed he had no shame.

It's clear that he was dangerous
And posed to them a threat.
They pondered if he could be bought
Or, maybe, better yet

What if they filled his heart with fear
And saw his role reversed?
What if they led him to believe
That he, himself, was cursed?

It was against their code to kill
So, that was not a choice.
But what if they should place a spell
That took away his voice?

The Fire

The Weston's house had caught on fire
And all had been afraid
The neighborhood's in jeopardy;
Disaster ready-made.

But when the firemen had arrived
They all had been amazed.
The fire, somehow, had been contained
And just that house had blazed.

They quickly had put out the fire
As it seemed self-contained.
Although there was some puzzlement
As questions still remained.

Within the crowd stood Marybeth
Who watched it all unfold.
Then when the crowd had been dispersed
A smile she could not hold.

Recent History

Throughout its recent history
Some odd things had occurred.
Though most of them went unexplained
Their mayor reassured

That explanations would be found
If patience they would show.
For there had been no mysteries
Just things they did not know.

But her people wanted answers
As fear began to grow.
For people become terrified
Of what they do not know.

And all these odd occurrences
Had put people on edge.
They feared the supernatural
As some now would allege.

The Doubts

The people had seemed very nice
And he was treated well.
But there were doubts that haunted him
That he could not dispel.

Though Rob had never been someone
Who wished to get involved.
There's something that had bothered him
In how this town evolved.

The rumors of the oddities
That sometimes had occurred
Had raised so little questioning
It seemed to be absurd.

Rob found it strange Lou's family
Had never been involved
With any of the mysteries
That had gone unresolved.

But all had seemed to be at peace
With how the town was run.
If there was one to question it,
He would not be the one.

Their History

In the past they called them witches
As they'd not understood
Those women with abilities
Were pledged to doing good.

So, if their secrets were revealed
The penalty came swift.
Their deaths were truly horrible
With mercy casted adrift.

But since they had been different
They sparked in people fear.
To where some created stories
Where evil they'd appear.

So now down through the centuries
They had been forced to hide.
As a lack of understanding
The reason why they died.

A Profile put in Action

Melissa saw they stared at her
Which had raised an alarm.
For she saw no admiration
But thoughts of doing harm.

His acolytes had researched her
As she fit the profile.
It was their wish to prove him right
By placing her on trial.

Melissa tried to get away
But they had given chase.
In panic she ran in the street
But she failed in her haste

To notice the oncoming bus
That had no time to break.
Although Melissa had been killed
They claimed it's by mistake.

The Paradox

The Preacher was a paradox
That was hard to define.
The things he claimed that he believed
And acts did not align.

He stood on his accomplishments
Though none had he achieved.
He'd offered them no evidence
And yet, they still believed.

He preyed upon their darkest fears
To draw them to his side.
Though any that had grown aware
He'd quickly cast aside.

He claimed he was their champion
But secretly had kept
The fact it was a power grab
Had been his main concept.

He was the master of deceit
Though claimed an open book.
And therein lies the paradox
Where things aren't how they look.

Payback

The crowd had reached a fevered pitch
Before he took the stage.
He preened before his audience
Prepared to vent his rage.

But when he spoke no sound emerged
And he looked mystified.
The crowd emitted one shocked gasp
Before the moment died.

His acolytes rushed him off stage
As panic had set in.
Where the crowd became unruly
As heads began to spin.

But amid all the confusion
It seemed that no one saw
The three members of the Chosen
And root of the faux pau.

The Disciple

Aaron Jones was his disciple
And his apparent heir.
None had ever seen the Preacher
When Aaron was not there.

But Aaron had a darker side
The Preacher had not known.
For Aaron kept it hidden well
So, rarely was it shown.

Though Aaron had embraced the cause
He still was well aware
The Preacher had some other plans
And soon would not be there.

So when the Preacher stepped aside
The cause would fall to him.
Then he would be the one to lead
And reaching out to them.

For he believed most fervently
In all the Preacher said.
For he was a true disciple
As on the cause he fed.

Parker Andrews' Disappearance

When Parker Andrews disappeared
The whole town was alarmed.
For she had been the sweetest Child
Who most had thought was charmed.

Miss Blackstone said she saw her leave
But not which way she went.
As there were tests she had to grade.
That's where her time was spent.

She disappeared right after school
So most would then assume
It happened when she turned for home
And, somehow, met her doom.

Police were called and searches made
But they had found no clue
To Parker Andrews' whereabouts
Or what she had been through.

The Change

This act had brought a change to town
That once had been archived.
The people acted diff'rently
From when he first arrived.

There now were petty arguments
And general discord.
As though a switch someone had flipped
Outside of their accord.

Where once they were oblivious
To what was happening
Or someone in authority
Was busy covering.

Regardless of the rationale
And all that had occurred
The people had grown sick of what
They found they now endured.

First Date

He dearly wished to ask her out
But move had not yet made.
As the thought of her rejection
Had left him quite afraid.

He faced rejection through his youth
Until he ran away.
But the streets had been no better
When people passed his way.

But then he thought, if she agreed
He knew little of her.
He had no clue what they would do
Or what she would prefer.

Though courage was in short supply
When Marybeth came by
He asked her if she liked the park
To which she had asked why.

He thought that, maybe, after work
She'd like to take a walk.
The park had seemed the perfect place
Where they could sit and talk.

His Story

His folks were fundamentalists
Who knew just wrong and right.
They never saw a shade of Grey
But only black and white.

His parents claimed he's Satan's spawn
The way he misbehaved.
Their rules they had strictly enforced
As though he was enslaved.

So he, his parents disavowed
And had abandoned him.
Because the only truth they saw
Was he brought shame to them.

The beatings were unbearable
And came more frequently.
So, he'd chosen to run away
Where from them he'd be free.

For months he called the streets his home
And struggled to survive.
But he was now completely free
And glad to be alive.

Lindsey

While Lindsey was an acolyte
She was the one he named.
He said he had the evidence.
At least, that's what he claimed.

Though Lindsey had denied the charge
The damage had been done.
The crowd had quickly turned on her
With hope of living, none.

They found her hanging in the square
Beneath the maple tree.
As she committed suicide
And hung for all to see.

She was not one of the Chosen
But victim who'd been played.
Now the Preacher had foundation
To launch his grand crusade.

Another Tragedy

Police called it an accident
But many were not sure.
The façade of the building fell
And reasons were obscure.

It happened as though by design
One Sunday afternoon.
With people taken by surprise
And lives taken too soon.

The carnage had been terrible
And rescue had been slow.
The Mayor called for volunteers
Michelle said both should go.

But none of them had been prepared
To see the damage done.
With mangled bodies ev'rywhere
Who found no place to run.

Although they did investigate
No reason did they find
To account for the accident
And grant all peace of mind.

Michelle's Mothering

Michelle had tried to mother him
But Rob seemed to resist.
For he'd not known a nurturer
Like Michelle could exist.

The concept of a family
Was something he'd not known.
For although he knew his parents
No love was ever shown.

He feared Michelle may smother him
So great was her concern
That someone should look after him
And it was now her turn.

And though he was appreciative
Of all that she had done.
He found that he had best been served
When he had trusted none.

A Change of Attitude

He watched the stars float overhead
Immersed in inner peace
When she approached him from the dark
All sultry and caprice.

Her manner had been different
Than what he'd seen before.
He'd always found her more reserved
And, sometimes, quite a bore.

But tonight she had been diff'rent
Which he had thought was strange.
As though something happened to her
That caused her heart to change.

Perhaps it merely was a tease
To see how he'd react.
But he found that he had liked it
And that was just a fact.

What had been Unseen

The stranger seemed to slip through town
As though he was a breeze.
He seemed to be invisible
To go where he would please.

In truth, a stranger should stand out
But he just blended in.
As none in the community
Could say where he had been.

Suspicions should have followed him
But that was not the case.
Somehow, it seemed, he had free reign
Though no one knew his face.

But none it seemed were curious
To why it was he came.
And even more disturbing was
That no one knew his name.

The Churches all were Full

It seemed the churches all were full
So great had been their fear.
As refuge had seemed paramount
In light of what was here.

They took no time to socialize.
In fact, none wished to leave.
As they prayed for sanctuary
That through church they'd receive.

But solace had been hard to find
In light of what occurred.
As the state of their survival
Could never be assured.

And so to church they all had flocked
As though a last resort.
Their faith was not what it should be.
In fact, it came up short.

At a Loss

The Chosen now were at a loss
For they could not explain
The evil that had gripped the town
And caused such grief and pain.

These evil acts came not from them
But from a source unknown.
It was a force outside of them
That plotted on its own.

They feared one stark reality.
Perhaps they'd been betrayed.
With Miss Blackstone so unstable
Perhaps on her it preyed.

The Chosen had been mortified
To be caught unaware.
For the scope of their assignment
Was always be aware.

When His Thoughts Would Turn to Her

He found his thoughts would turn to her
When he would least expect.
As though she'd placed a spell on him
That forced him to reflect.

She clearly could be obstinate
But, also, she was strong.
It's her demure exterior
Where people judged her wrong.

She had a great capacity
For how much she could care.
Her courage was unnatural
As nothing she won't dare.

But she was also secretive
Which had stirred his concern.
For what it was he did not know
He was afraid to learn.

The Complaints

The mayor had received complaints
The Preacher's lost control.
The crowds that now had followed him
Saw vengeance as a goal.

For each misfortune that they'd faced
The crowd now placed the blame
On anyone the Preacher dared
To point to and to name.

The crowd whipped into a frenzy
By his outrageous claims
For fear had swept throughout the town
As to who next he names.

Most feared the crowds were dangerous
Just waiting to explode.
While the Preacher primed the trigger
And stood at the crossroad.

The Fireman's Fair

The highlight of the calendar
Had been the Fireman's Fair.
Which ev'ry one looked forward to
The one week it was there.

And Marybeth had wished to go
But would not go alone.
So, she asked Rob if he'd join her.
He would, but hid his groan.

He thought these fairs were ludicrous
And greatly overpriced.
Where only suckers went to them
Who're easily enticed.

But he found he was mistaken
For, truly, he had fun.
They even tried some gaming booths
Where teddy bear he'd won.

When they were done, he walked her home
But when he turned to leave
Marybeth had dared to kiss him
So hard he could not breathe.

The Rumors

The rumors had been hard to quell
With all the mystery.
It all seemed supernatural
To the community.

The tragedies they had endured
They felt were undeserved.
It was a good community
That should have been preserved.

But rumors now were on the rise
With ev'ry incident.
For someone was responsible
Who prowled with bad intent.

While rumors found it possible
A witch could be at fault.
If one could be identified
They'd justify assault.

The Sign

When Lou asked Rob to fix the sign
That hung above the store.
Rob had simply placed the ladder
Unmindful of the door.

So, while he was two stories high
The opened door had hit
The ladder that had blocked the door
Upon a blind exit.

Rob lost his balance and he fell
With death a surety.
When something strange slowed his descent
And landed him softly.

He noticed Marybeth was there
As footing he regained.
And asked her what she thought she saw
Which could not be explained.

She said she saw him float in air
As though he's a balloon.
But for where he'd placed the ladder,
He seemed like a buffoon.

The Unexplainable

For days he had reflected on
The strangeness that occurred.
It's clear to him he should be dead.
Of that he was assured.

What happened was a miracle
Which still had shocked his brain.
With Marybeth, he was quite sure,
Unable to explain.

Perhaps it had been providence
That interfered with fate.
For, otherwise, he had no clue
Why death he'd still await.

It's beyond his comprehension
To explain what occurred
But he had been truly grateful
His death had been deferred.

The Dream

The dream he dreamed had never seemed
He had been worthy of.
But now that he'd found Marybeth
He wondered if it's love.

For love he'd never known before.
His parents had not cared.
And, clearly, when he roamed the streets
There's none there who had dared.

He could not wipe her from his thoughts
And his dreams, she'd invade.
He would get this funny feeling
When eye contact was made.

He had never known the passion
That now he seemed to feel.
Though he had wondered to himself
If this was even real.

The Bridge Collapse

The bridge collapse had killed a score
And bred hysteria.
For once again the reasons sought
Lacked true criteria.

There had been claims that its supports
Had simply given way.
But engineers refuted that.
The bridge was built to stay.

Some claimed an act of sabotage
But no one could explain
Exactly what was done to it
To place it under strain.

So, there was no explanation
That seemed to satisfy
The answers that the people sought
To who it was and why.

The Preacher's Aspirations

The Preacher had aspirations
Beyond his Grand Crusade.
For that merely was the platform
On which his future laid.

For he'd run for public office
And be the people's choice.
Where he had planned to promise them
That he would be their voice.

For those who were his followers
Would give him their support.
And any error that he made
He knew they'd not report.

So now he thought his path would lead
Where fortune and fame wait.
And all because he understood
How much they liked to hate.

Suspicions

Suspicions had been running high
As none knew whom to trust.
Where even close relationships
Were showing signs of rust.

It seemed the sexes were at war
Which may have been his goal.
Relationships are built on trust
And lack had took its toll.

It always seems the innocent
Are those who have to pay.
When evil rears its ugly head
At the end of the day.

Now people were afraid to meet
Despite how they may feel.
Suspicions made it dangerous
And the threat very real.

The Beast

The beast despised the witches too
For reasons of its own.
As it's the goodness in their souls
For which they must atone.

It seemed the crusade roused the beast
And led it straight to them.
The clergy claimed it was the beast
The Preacher should condemn.

The Preacher would have none of it
And called the clergy fools.
It's obvious a witch's spell
Had turned them into tools.

Then to his many followers
The Preacher had proclaimed
The beast was just a fantasy
The Preacher had disclaimed.

Tranquility

He'd never known tranquility
As he had found with her.
Perhaps, at last, he'd found a home
Where he could feel secure.

His heart would race when she came near
Like it had not before.
But that also brought comforting
That struck him to his core.

She'd never chained him with demands
But pulled from him his best.
She appeared the destination
Of what had been his quest.

In her he found tranquility
That he had never known.
Now she was ev'rything to him
And he was not alone.

They Found Parker Andrews

They discovered Parker Andrews
Though those who found her cried.
For she'd been dead for sev'ral days
And none knew why she died.

It was clear she'd been brutalized
For reasons none could guess.
Her parents were beside themselves
So great was their distress.

The town in its entirety
Had been shocked to the core.
And it seemed the Preacher's message
Attracted more and more.

The people came to speculate
The town had become hell.
It seemed the town was targeted
By some unholy spell.

Marybeth's Secret

One night a week she would sneak off
To where, she would not say.
And she'd become so secretive
It rubbed him the wrong way.

Rob asked her once where she would go
But he got no reply.
As though the question was not asked
So she'd no need to lie.

One night, Rob dared to follow her
To find what she concealed.
But he was taken by surprise
In what had been revealed.

He came upon a gathering
Of women in a glade
Who're performing a ritual
That left him sore afraid.

He prayed they had not spotted him
As he had slipped away.
But wondered who the women were
That had been on display.

The Questions

Rob had waited throughout the night
For Marybeth's return.
He was burning for the answers
He was afraid to learn.

He saw there was much more to her
Than what he had believed.
He'd found she had a secret life
And felt he'd been deceived.

Who were those women she was with
And what were they about?
He prayed nothing nefarious
But could not quell his doubts.

His heart had told him he should trust
But he had found it hard
Because the secrets that she kept
Had shown him no regard.

The Confrontation

When Rob had first confronted her
Marybeth was surprised.
She saw he felt he was betrayed
As pain he'd not disguised.

She wished she could apologize
But then she must confess
She had been one of the Chosen
Which she could not address.

But Rob read in her reluctance
A lack of faith in him.
Which he said had only proven
There was no hope for them.

Perhaps it's time that he moved on
With welcome overstayed.
He could not dodge the feeling that
He merely had been played.

Then Marybeth began to cry
Before she ran away.
He knew he made a huge mistake
But not meant it that way.

A Meeting of the Minds

As Rob approached, Lou came to him
And said she's really mad.
She locked herself inside her room.
So it was pretty bad.

Emotions got the best of her
And he had been the cause.
He had thrown out accusations
As though grasping at straws.

It was never his intention
To cause her this distress.
But it seemed that he was callous
And the source of this mess.

He spoke to her outside her door
And begged her to forgive.
He knew he was insensitive
As it's her life to live.

But the feeling that came to him
He'd never felt before.
And the feeling made him crazy
Not knowing what it's for.

Then Marybeth opened the door
And locked him in embrace.
The move had caught him by surprise
As she had kissed his face.

If they wished a relationship
They had to learn to trust.
And she needed assurances
When trouble was a must

His first thought's not to run away
Not think of their welfare.
For she would never think to run
Because she'd dared to care.

For that had been his history
When things grew difficult.
The highway was his first response
And now as a result

She feared to place her faith in him
Then have him run away.
She had need of his commitment
No matter what, he'd stay.

To all of it he had agreed
Except for one small glitch.
He looked directly in her eyes
And asked if she's a witch.

A Lost Argument

How could he lose an argument
While knowing he was right.
It had not even been his choice
As she began the fight.

And ev'ry point he hoped to make
She had turned back on him.
As though she was the injured one
And he's the true problem.

He was upset with secrets kept
If help he could provide.
But she had claimed he was upset
Because she hurt his pride.

He saw there's not the slightest hope
That he could win this fight.
How could he lose the argument
When he was clearly right.

How's a Witch Defined?

She said it all depended on
How witch he would define.
The source of her abilities
Had truly been divine.

Through faith the Lord had chosen them
To carry out His will.
And each of them had sworn an oath
His will they would fulfill.

And that was what they'd thought they'd done
Until just recently.
For now, there was a force in town
That scared them terribly.

She believed that she'd been chosen
To face a special threat.
But what it was she had not known.
At least, that is, not yet.

A Voice of Reason

The mayor stood before the crowd
With reason as her goal.
Perhaps she'd put an end to this.
At least, regain control.

"We cannot live our lives in fear
Or else we cease to live.
The harm that has been done to us
We somehow must forgive."

"For our vengeance brings us nothing
To mitigate our strife.
As tragedies occur to us
For that's a part of life."

"To allow our fears to own us
Is simply giving in.
We should be made of sterner stuff
Than what we've lately been."

She saw that half the crowd agreed.
The other half did not.
Although she tried pure reasoning
She may have missed the spot.

The Magic

He asked from where the magic came.
She thought before reply.
Her answer he'd find difficult
But she'd give it a try.

The magic lived within them all
But most choose to ignore.
So fearful of discovery
They will not dare explore.

The insights that are there to gain
Most people fail to find.
Because of limits self-imposed
Which serves to make them blind.

But for those who had been chosen
Those limits don't apply.
For the Chosen were enlightened
As on faith they'd rely.

What He could never Tell Her

He could not tell her to her face
As he had felt some shame.
However she defined herself
His feelings were the same.

If everything she told him
Had proved to be a lie.
His feelings for her would not change
Though he could not say why.

He'd like to think that it was trust
But knew that can't be right.
He'd never trusted anyone
Nor with one been forthright.

She may prove herself a monster
And, truly, he'd not care.
She even could pretend to him
As long as she was there.

True Intent

Soon the Preacher grew suspicious
Of Aaron's true intent.
Although he swore his loyalty
His passion was absent.

He feared that Aaron's not the man
That he had claimed to be.
Having underlying motives
No one's allowed to see.

Though he claimed to be disciple
There was something not right.
He'd now challenge authority
And often slipped from sight.

There'd been a subtle change in him
That was hard to define.
And he'd begun questioning
With whom he would align.

Miss Blackstone's Charge

Miss Blackstone came into the shop
But it was not to buy.
Instead, she looked for Marybeth
To ask the question why.

For Miss Blackstone blamed Marybeth
For all that had occurred.
Claiming Marybeth was a witch
Whose evil had endured.

The woman grew hysterical
The more she'd rant and raved.
Screaming Marybeth had to die
If they were to be saved.

Then Rob had forced her from the store
Believing she was ill.
But left her standing on the street
Where she became more shrill.

Till, finally, police arrived
And carted her away.
While Marybeth just stared at him
Not knowing what to say.

Whatever's Unexplainable

Sometimes we find we're quick to judge
Before we know what's true.
And thus, we find we're incorrect
In how we follow through.

The age-old story still holds true;
In fear of the unknown
Whatever's unexplainable
We've no wish to be shown.

So, the conclusions that we reach
We do so out of fear.
Whatever's unexplainable
We've no wish to go near.

We lament opportunities
That we have somehow missed
Because it's unexplainable
The chance we had dismissed.

The Preacher's Wife

They found her hanging in the square
Devoid of any life.
The crowd it seemed was mesmerized
To see the Preacher's wife.

Someone proclaimed she was a witch
The Preacher tried to hide.
Perhaps it was she felt betrayed
And that's why she had died.

The Preacher seemed to be in shock
As he just stood and stared.
His wife was such a gentle soul
But for this unprepared.

When Marybeth went up to him
He turned and ran away.
But Marybeth had given chase
To help him in some way.

Though there're many who had doubted
The scene that they had eyed.
For few believed she was the type
To commit suicide.

Remorse

When Marybeth discovered him
He looked as though he'd cried.
Because the truth he found in her
He publicly denied.

He saw the goodness in her heart
And simply turned away.
His aspirations tugged at him
And over him held sway.

He knew he was responsible
For most that had occurred.
The terror that he'd instigate
He now saw as absurd.

Forgiveness seemed too much to ask
Now that his wife was dead.
For someone stole his Grand Crusade
And this was where it led.

The Preacher's Body

The Preacher's body was displayed
And posed for all to see.
As though a message had been sent
Like it was meant to be.

The ghastly sight had stirred the pot
As all were terrified.
It seemed that ev'ryone in town
Already charged and tried.

It seemed the witches got to him
As that was Aaron's claim.
A witch that's unidentified
Or one he'd yet to name.

And like a tropic hurricane
His death became a storm.
As Aaron then had claimed the throne
Which caused rumors to swarm.

Disregarding Consequence

There was no justice nor a peace
For those that he had named.
As his minions grew so mindless
No act would leave them shamed.

He disregarded consequence
With each outlandish claim.
Not caring what the fate may be
For any that he'd name.

He named the town librarian
Which drew a gasp of breath.
Two days later someone found her
And she'd been stoned to death.

Although Aaron had been questioned
He claimed he did not know
Who may have been responsible
To that extreme would go.

Jill

A crowd had formed outside her house
Which had caused Jill concern.
She'd never heard of the crusade
And had no wish to learn.

Her name was one that Aaron fed
Unto his multitude.
So when Jill had confronted them
The crowd turned cold and rude.

They chased her back inside her house
Where she huddled in fear.
Though when police dispersed the crowd
She still did not appear.

When they had knocked upon her door
Jill had failed to respond.
So, they had forced their way inside
To find she was beyond

The help that they hoped to provide
For she was clearly dead.
It seemed someone slipped from the crowd
And then bashed in her head.

The Meeting

He met her in an alleyway
Just as she had prescribed.
Where she told him her suspicions
Though logic they defied.

But Miss Blackstone had assured him
That all she said was true.
She had refused to tell him how
But trust her that she knew.

Though Aaron still looked skeptical
Miss Blackstone did persist.
A darkness had come over them
That they could not resist.

But though he took her at her word
Something had not seemed right.
As though she was a chandelier
Where just one bulb would light.

The Tinderbox

The Mayor's people were dismayed
Since Aaron gained control.
The crowds had grown more boisterous
With all that he'd extol.

They told her it's a tinderbox
Just waiting to explode.
As ev'ry odd thing that occurred
Caused faith in her erode.

Each incident he now would say
Gave proof to what he claimed.
And cases of assaults had climbed
Towards any that he named.

Though violence he'd not incite
He never called for calm.
But it seemed that his followers
Were edgy as a bomb.

Perhaps these were the warning signs
Of what was yet to come.
Already they had faced so much
And forced to overcome.

The Mayor's Worry

The mayor began to worry
That things were out of hand.
Now Aaron's staging spectacles
That were both dark and grand.

The allegations that he made
Had bordered on insane.
But still had grown his following
Which she believed inane.

These acts were not coincidence
But rather had seemed planned.
As though there'd been some force at work
Where the town had been damned.

Now constituents had clamored
That something must be done.
The whole town was apoplectic
And felt under the gun.

The Stranger Walked Among Them

Though the stranger walked among them
He seemed to walk unseen.
For none who viewed the tragedies
Had claimed that he'd been seen.

He made sure that none had noticed
The places he had been.
As he moved amid the shadows
No other would go in.

He was like an apparition
Who'd suddenly appear.
Then without a moment's notice
Would quickly disappear.

Though they found him quite suspicious
They'd not the slightest clue
That he had been involved with this
Although it may be true.

This Madness had to End

She'd bring this madness to an end,
Or so the Mayor thought.
The situation's out of hand
As hate was all he brought.

His crowds could quickly turn to mobs
Just ready to rampage.
They clung to Aaron's rhetoric
Which filled them with more rage.

The Mayor felt this had to stop
And Aaron was the key.
She now suspicioned he was not
Who he had claimed to be.

She had known he had a rally
That's scheduled for that night.
Which she intended to attend
And try to set things right.

The Children of the Damned

They were the children of the damned
Was how Aaron began.
An evil had awoken here
That threatened ev'ry man.

For years it laid in dormancy
But now it had returned.
There was a coven in the town
That must be flushed and burned.

The crowd had reached a fevered pitch
With Aaron in control.
He saw pure chaos may erupt
And still he would cajole.

The Mayor tried confronting him
But he casted her aside.
The Mayor landed awkwardly
And suffered while she died.

He pointed then to Marybeth
And claimed she was a witch.
So they, on his authority,
Should kill the evil bitch.

When Marybeth he named a witch
Lou leapt to her defense.
But the mob was uncontrollable
And anger did dispense.

Rob wondered if Lou always knew
The truth of Marybeth
Or had it merely come to him
The moment of his death.

The crowd then turned on Marybeth
With her guilt now assured.
And they would dole out punishment
With anything procured.

She looked at Rob with pleading eyes
That screamed she was afraid.
For now, that she'd been targeted
Her fate was clearly laid.

Rob fought them off the best he could
But he was overmatched.
He cried for Marybeth to run
As he still clawed and scratched.

But she would not abandon him
Though faced a paradox.
To help she must reveal herself
And thus, Pandora's box.

She stood as though a warrior
Who was prepared for war.
A woman of true confidence
He had not seen before.

She felt she had but one good choice
So, put on a display.
As with a single wave she had
Swept all of them away.

It's then the beast had been unleashed
And stood for all to see.
As Aaron's merely a disguise
And now the beast was free.

It leaped as though an animal.
Its target, Marybeth.
But Rob had dared to intercede
To challenge certain death.

It never was his wish to die
But if it was to be
The only way he'd welcome it
If Marybeth went free.

The beast had grabbed him by the throat
To where he could not breathe.
He stared into its blood red eyes
And felt its anger seethe.

He faced his own mortality
And knew that it was true.
The fate that had awaited him
Had long been overdue.

When Marybeth came to his aid
The beast had first recoiled.
As though the carnage it had sought
She, maybe, could have foiled.

But then composure it reclaimed
As Marybeth it struck.
The blow had caught her by surprise
When she'd no chance to duck.

The Chosen then revealed themselves
As this was judgment day.
A demon had come unto them
That they were sworn to slay.

The Chosen then unleashed the force
That they'd held in reserve.
The beast had been no match for it
And quickly lost its nerve.

Now desperate for an escape
It found nowhere to run.
So, it turned and charged the Chosen
Prepared to spare no one.

The Chosen were not physical.
Some fell to its attack.
But they'd other abilities
They employed to fight back.

Where like a wounded animal
It howled in its dismay.
As it succumbed to their power
And slowly passed away.

As Rob had crawled to Marybeth
He saw that she was hurt.
He prayed it was not serious
Though she'd not seemed alert.

He heard the cheers, and thus assumed
The demon now was dead.
As he attended Marybeth
While he, himself had bled.

Her eyes were holding at half mast
As he just shook his head.
He thought it pretty obvious
That soon she would be dead.

She looked at him but could not speak
Though mouthed her love was true.
He gently kissed her on the lips
And said he loved her too.

He held her in his arms and cried
As he'd not cried before.
He knew that she was lost to him
Though he had wanted more.

The crowd had stared in disbelief
At what had just occurred.
It seemed the evil brought to them
They had, themselves, assured.

Michelle had forced the crowd to part
Then stared in disbelief.
She blamed them all for what occurred
Then crumpled in her grief.

Sometimes the angels of the Lord
Are not what we expect.
So, when they may appear to us
Those angels we reject.

Recovery

Rob woke to find Michelle was there
And all his wounds were dressed.
She said he's lucky to survive
And that he should feel blessed.

She said it took them quite a while
To figure it all out.
It seemed the stranger was the beast
With Aaron just a scout.

And it appeared Aaron was killed
When he fulfilled his role.
The beast then chose him as disguise,
The crusade to control.

Rob languished in recovery
More than he would have liked.
Some days he thought he'd be okay.
Some days his heartbreak spiked.

When he'd ask about the Chosen
She'd pretend not to hear.
For all of them that had survived
Had seemed to disappear.

A Dark Place

It was a dark place where he went
So great had been his grief.
The fact that he had done his best
Provided no relief.

He told Michelle in confidence
The dark place he was in.
He never had known love before
And may not love again.

She'd been a beacon to the world
Like none he'd ever known.
And bravely she'd stood by her faith
Where doubts were never shown.

It was a dark place where he went
As anger claimed his heart.
He wanted vengeance for her death
But knew not where to start.

But then he thought, what would she say
If Marybeth had known.
The dark place he took refuge in
She never would condone.

Remaining Questions

There were some questions that remained
Rob felt he had to know.
If all the Chosen disappeared
Where was it they would go?

Why was it they'd abandon them
After what they'd been through?
Perhaps it was they felt betrayed
Which the town can't undo.

He felt Michelle ignoring him
As she did not respond.
The questions really bothered him
And could not get beyond.

The word had been they disappeared
As they'd planned all along.
Michelle then turned and winked at him.
Perhaps the word was wrong.

Epilog

Michelle asked Rob if he'd stay on
For now that Lou was gone
She could not run the store alone
But needed to move on.

But Rob replied, it may be best
If he took to the road.
Her loss had hit him very hard
And he faced overload.

Though they had been like family.
The only one he'd known.
He found with both of them now dead
He's once again alone.

Then he read her disappointment
And knew she's hurting too.
His thoughts had flashed to Marybeth
And knew what he must do.

It did not happen overnight
But sometime and somehow
They again became family
And had each other now.

THE CHOSEN

a poetic novel by Gordon Bostic

In a serene American town where reality and the mystical intertwine, "The Chosen"
is a mesmerizing tale of love, magic, and human resilience. When a runaway named
Rob disrupts the tranquil facade, the lives of the townsfolk are forever changed.
Through well-crafted characters and poetic prose, this enchanting novel explores
the extraordinary within the ordinary, blurring the boundaries between what is real
and what is magical. As strange occurrences unfold, a hidden world of destiny and
wonder emerges, captivating readers with suspense and intrigue. At its core, "The
Chosen" is a celebration of love's transformative power, the strength of community,
and the enduring nature of hope. With its beautifully developed characters and
evocative language, Author Gordon Bostic invites you to reflect on your own lives,
urging to embrace the magic that exists within and believes in the extraordinary
potential of every individual. This captivating journey lingers in the heart, leaving a
lasting impression and generating substantial interest in the literary landscape.

ABOUT THE AUTHOR:

Gordon Bostic was born in West Virginia and grew up in
Virginia. He's a graduate of Dabney S. Lancaster Community
College, James Madison University, Brookdale Community
College and Fairleigh Dickinson University. He worked as
a computer scientist and a software engineer for most of his
life. He began writing at a young age as a way of expressing
himself, his feelings, and his view of the world. He has
currently had seven books published. Gordon currently lives on the Jersey Shore
with his wife, Susan.

www.ingramcontent.com/pod-product-compliance
Lightning Source LLC
Chambersburg PA
CBHW030820200726
48288CB00004B/1310